Have You Seen My Friends?

The Adventures of Creativity

Written by
Monica H. Kang

Illustrated by **Khadeeja Qureshi**

Halo
alo
PUBLISHING
INTERNATIONAL

Hey there,
friendly ones,
I'm looking for my friends.

I think they are lost.
Have you seen them by chance?

Oh, what are they like?
Thank you for asking.
Allow me to share.

Curiosity is the silly one,
asking lots of questions.

Courage is
the brave one,
always trying
something new.

Creativity is
the imaginative one,
always finding the way
when we are lost.

They used to be everywhere and anywhere.

We sure were a good team, making every mess an opportunity and brightening everyone's days with more possibilities.

Curiosity is an inquisitive mind, hungry to learn and encourages us to wander and wonder what else may be out there.

Courage is an open heart, hungry to listen and encourages us to explore the unfamiliar and face our fears.

Creativity is a bubbly and energetic soul, hungry to encourage us to imagine different ways of doing things - even when others say no.

They may look similar, but they are different indeed.

We sure were a good team.

They changed shapes and sizes while staying true to who they were at heart and brought rainbows when others saw darkness.

Yes, perhaps you have seen them.
They seem to hang out around
friends like you—kind,
welcoming and real.

Oh, how did I lose them?
What a good question, my dear.
Allow me to share.

I can't remember exactly when and where it happened.
I just woke up one day and my three friends were gone.

What I do know is that the more I tried to fit in, the harder it was to see my friends and the more scared I became just to be me.

I thought I didn't need to play with them as much.

I had so much work and so many responsibilities and expectations to meet.

I thought growing older meant being serious all the time, and that I had no more room for them in my life.

But as I woke up feeling gloomy, I realized I was wrong. No matter how old I am, I need these friends in my life.

For they are the nicest friends you could have. As people of all ages would say, being curious, courageous and creative gives us more life to live each day.

So now I am on a quest
to find them, and ask you:
Have you seen my friends,
curiosity, courage and
creativity, by chance?

Just ask, you say.
I hadn't thought of that.
    Maybe if I find the courage
    to ask "Where are you?"
    Then I can find them.

There you are, my dear lost friends!
I didn't realize you were here all along!

Thank you for being here even
when I felt doubt, and coming back
to shine more brightly each day.

What is that you say? Oh, would you like to play with our friends together today? That would most certainly be an honor, my friends, because you and your friends helped me find my friends again.

The more the merrier, they say:
when all of our friends are here to stay,
friends who let us be ourselves,
friends who let us feel all of our feelings
and treasure our time together.

I am so happy that
I found my friends again.

What about you?

The End

For my parents and friends
who never gave up on me when I felt lost.

ISBN Paperback: 978-1-63765-128-5
ISBN Hardcover: 978-1-63765-127-8
LCCN: 2021919835

Halo Publishing International, LLC
www.halopublishing.com

Printed and bound in the United States of America

Author

Monica H. Kang wonders how we can all live each day with more color and possibilities. As an award-winning author and Founder of InnovatorsBox®, she is on a mission to unlock creativity for all. She once thought she lost her dear friends too and hopes that this book inspires you to never part with your precious friends in your adventures. When curious Monica isn't traveling, she lives in Washington, D.C. daydreaming of more possibilities with her friends.

Visit www.creativitywithmonica.com for more resources.

Illustrator

Khadeeja Qureshi loves to tell stories by illustrating magical dreamy landscapes. She started drawing fantasy illustrations from a young age as she grew up in Peshawar, Pakistan. Today she continues to bring out more magic through her illustrations as a children's book illustrator.

InnovatorsBox®

InnovatorsBox is on a mission to unlock creativity for all. We dedicate this book and the series of "The Adventures of Creativity" to help more young and old friends reconnect with their curiosity, courage and creativity everyday no matter where you are. Thank you for painting more possibilities by being you every day.

CPSIA information can be obtained
at www.ICGtesting.com
Printed in the USA
BVRC102340041121
619989BV00001BA/3